CW00840070

She Died on a Monday

Kevin McLeod

Copyright 2021 Kevin McLeod

For Rachael and Elena.

She died on a Monday. No long lingering illness. No last words, just there, then gone. One minute they were sharing breakfast, the next his world collapsed. She was falling too fast and he was moving too slow. Later, the doctor would tell him that it didn't matter how fast he had moved. He couldn't have saved her. Like that makes it ok. As if that would make him feel better. It mattered to him. He should have caught her and helped her; instead he had moved in slow motion as the love of his life, his very reason for living, disappeared in front of his eyes.

There was no warning. She had been healthy and happy. Ten minutes before she died, they had been discussing what to do after breakfast. He remembered scoffing at her suggestion that they should visit his sister. He tried to remember the last words he had said to her. Finally, they came back to him. Is there any toast? Such a normal question, but now it seemed so stupid, so banal. If he had known they were going to be his last words to her he would have said something meaningful, something profound.

Later, the doctor would tell him that it had been an aneurysm in her brain and that she had felt no pain. Should this comfort him? If it was supposed to, it didn't. Somehow the suddenness made it worse. Neither of them had been prepared for this. The numbness he felt began cocooning him in his own sorrow.

At some point, he didn't remember when, his daughter arrived. She was talking to the medical crew. She turned and began to talk to him. He couldn't make out the words. The lines of her face were blurred by his tears and her words were unable to penetrate an overwhelming numbness.

They took his wife's body away, carted it off on a trolley like she was nothing. He wanted to yell at them, to make them do this terrible thing in some different way. Instead, he sat and watched while his daughter hugged him. He was vaguely aware he wasn't hugging her back, his arms unwilling to move.

He found himself on the couch, unaware of how he had come to be there. His daughter was on the phone and his son had arrived. His son was looking in drawers and speaking, but he couldn't make sense of it. He heard the word funeral and slowly his brain began to understand. His son was looking for the funeral plan papers. He managed to tell him where to find them. His voice was quiet, broken, as he mumbled through the words. His son put a hand on his shoulder and gave it a gentle squeeze. A simple act of love from a son to his father. He put his hand over his son's. No words were said.

He couldn't accept it, wouldn't accept it. His wife couldn't be dead. They had so many plans. So much to do. How could she be gone? They were due to go on holiday next month. It was all paid for and arranged. She had been looking forward to it. They both had. Now, they would never get to see those views, or take that boat trip. The same one they had taken on their first holiday together.

After a few hours of helping and being there for him, his son and daughter left. His daughter had asked to stay with him tonight, or for him to come with her, but he wanted to be alone. He managed to thank them for helping, while ushering them towards the door. He shut the door, instantly becoming aware of the silence. It crashed into him like a wave. There were no sounds coming from the kitchen, or from the radio in the living room. She always liked to listen to the same channel, keeping it on for some background noise. He walked to the living room and switched on the radio, as if this would bring her back. Feeling foolish, he turned it off again.

He lay down on the couch and cried himself to sleep.

'John, wake up, it's time to get up.'

He heard her voice so clearly that he woke with a start and sat up straight. Confusion took over as he tried to work out whether it had been a dream or if he had actually heard her voice. He looked to the large window, the one with her favourite view over the city from their fourth-floor apartment. It was one of the reasons they had bought this place, she loved that view. It must be late, as darkness had replaced light while he was sleeping. He turned on a lamp and went to shut the curtains. He froze, as just for a second, he swore that he saw her behind him. He turned to the living room but found only emptiness.

He drew the curtains and went to the kitchen. The clock on the wall told him it was a quarter past ten at night. He hadn't eaten all day and knew that he should. He went to the fridge and found a sandwich that his daughter must have made for him. He sat at the table, the same table where she had died, and stared at her empty space. Slowly, he ate the sandwich, tasting nothing.

He walked through the hall to their bedroom. Sitting on the edge of the bed, he stared at her side. Suddenly he felt it, her touch. He couldn't explain it, but he felt her. She was here, she was with him. But, as quickly as the sensation came, it left. His mind was playing tricks on him. It surely was understandable; he was processing the enormity of what had happened. He didn't bother to undress. Lying down on the bed, on top of the covers, he curled into the foetal position and began to cry.

She died on a Monday.

Tuesday

He woke up in the same position. For a few
blissful seconds, his mind let him forget the
horror of the previous day. He turned to
reach out to her and remembered. The pain
swept over him as his tears flowed freely. He
looked into the ensuite bathroom through
blurred eyes. He caught his breath and felt
his heart jump to his throat. Just for a
second, for a fleeting moment, he was sure
that he saw her in the mirror.

Staggering to his feet he went to the
bathroom but there was no one there. What
did he expect? He sighed deeply and
breathed in. He could smell her in this room.
Her perfume, her soap. The towels were
folded the way that she liked them and
arranged in order of size. She always kept
everything just the way she liked it. The way
he liked it.

He sat on the bathroom floor hugging one of
the towels and slowly quietened his tears.
His breathing became normal and silence
returned. He heard the music coming from
the living room. Had he left the radio on? He
didn't remember. Maybe his daughter had let
herself in. He wanted to be alone, he knew
his daughter meant well, but he needed time

and space. He would go through to the living room and let her know, as nicely as possible, that he wanted, needed, to be alone.

It took all his strength to stand and walk. Slowly, unsteadily, he stumbled from the bathroom, through the bedroom, and out into the hall. He could hear the radio clearly now. His wife's favourite channel was playing the tune of the gardening show she listened to every Tuesday. Did his daughter not realise how that music would make him feel? Did she have no concept of his pain? He felt his anger bubble as he opened the door to the living room.

Standing at the radio, with her back to him, was Elizabeth, his wife. He tried to speak, tried to move, but was unable to do either. Finally, his legs responded and he took two steps towards her, but she didn't turn to face him. He could almost touch her. He reached out just as the doorbell sounded. He looked briefly towards the front door and when he turned back, she was gone. Tears welled in his eyes; the pain in his heart seemed to grow. He didn't understand this. Was she here?

He heard keys in the door and then his daughter was calling his name as she walked towards the living room. She saw him standing in the middle of the room looking confused, with tears streaming down his face. His daughter rushed to him, putting her arms around him and this time he hugged back, sobbing uncontrollably into her hair.

They stood like that until his sobbing became quiet. He pulled away from his daughter and looked into her eyes. He smiled sadly and nodded his head. She smiled back and wiped her own tears away from her cheeks. It was easy for him to forget, while consumed by his own pain, that his children had also lost their mother.

His daughter asked if he had had any breakfast, while also explaining that his son would be in later. They had to go to the funeral place on Brook Street and to the church to begin arrangements. He nodded in silent understanding, while staring at the empty space in front of the radio. She had been right there; he had seen her.

They ate breakfast and his daughter did her best to fill the silences with meaningless small talk. He knew he should be saying more, should be contributing to the conversation, but he had no words. Time and time again, his thoughts reminded him that his daughter had lost her mum, just as suddenly as he had lost his wife. But somewhere between thought and speech, the words became lost, and he sat silently chasing his food around his plate.

After breakfast, his daughter asked him if he would like to change his clothes and take a shower. He realised he was still wearing yesterday's clothes. His shirt and trousers looked crumpled and slept in. Elizabeth would have been annoyed at his appearance. She always prided herself on her own, always wanted them both to look their best. You never knew who might come over she would say. He thought of it as nagging, but now he would give anything to hear her say it one more time.

Through in the bedroom, he sat on the bed and began to undress. His daughter had turned on the shower for him and had left a towel lying out. She said something he didn't quite catch and shut the door, leaving him to shower in peace.

Stepping into the warm water he didn't want to admit that it felt nice against his skin. It was like he didn't believe he should feel anything other than pain just now. Why should he feel warmth when she could feel nothing at all? His wife had died just over 24 hours ago, was it right he was doing anything other than grieving?

After 10 minutes of standing completely still in the shower, he finally gave in and washed properly. Turning the shower off and opening the door, he reached for his towel and dabbed at the water running down his face. He looked across into the steam filled mirror and there she was. His wife stood smiling at him from the mirror. He wiped his face again, as more water escaped from his hair, running into his eyes. When he removed the towel, she was gone.

Was this part of the process? Was his brain refusing to let go? He looked back at the mirror several times, but she didn't reappear. After he finished drying, he went through to the bedroom and started to get dressed.

He re-joined his daughter in the living room. His son would be here soon, and they would need to discuss funeral arrangements. His daughter asked if she should look out clothes for Elizabeth to be buried in. The question drove home the realisation; she's gone. He hasn't been seeing her around their apartment, she's gone and there's nothing he can do to bring her back. He began to cry; his daughter came around the table and hugged him tightly.

His son arrived and they discussed arrangements, what type of flowers, what music to play, and the catering for after the service. He tried to contribute to the conversation, tried to remember what flowers she liked, what music she would want, and what picture of her he wanted on the order of service.

His daughter asked if he would like to stay with her and again, politely, he refused. He promised he would look for a photo and for clothes for Elizabeth. His children left, and he was alone with the silence.

He stood at the window for a minute, looking out at the city. The people below were going about their daily routines. No one down there would notice that there was one more space in the crowd. Their worlds were untouched, while his was crumbling around him.

He stepped away from the window, silently cursing those below him, and went through to the bedroom. He opened her wardrobe and stood looking at Elizabeth's clothes. She had so many, so many outfits that he loved to see her in. He reached out to touch some of them, running his hand over several different options, but he couldn't decide which to choose. What do you bury the love of your life in?

He saw the outfit she had worn on their last anniversary. Remembered dancing with her and the joy of that night. This was the outfit he would choose. Smart and dressy, yet elegant at the same time. He laid it on the bed.

'I never really liked the jacket.'

Her voice came from behind him. He turned around as quickly as he could, but there was no one there. He shook his head as confusion took over. Was his mind playing tricks on him? He looked at the jacket again, but could see nothing wrong with it.

I like it, he said to the empty room. It reminds me of you at a happy time, he continued. He waited for a response, but there was none, what did he expect? Did he expect her to come running out of the bathroom and tell him several reasons that his choice was incorrect?

Next, he chose shoes. Simple black ones without a heel. They looked comfortable. Did that matter? He decided that it did. She always complained that high heels made her feet ache.

Happy with his choice, he opened the walk-in wardrobe and took out the small set of steps that allowed him to reach the top shelf. He found the box he was looking for and carefully took it down. Carrying the box through to the kitchen, he put it on the table and lifted the lid. Inside, the box was full of photos. Years and years of their life together. How did you choose just one?

He began looking through the box and reliving each photo that he picked up. From their early days, right up to their last holiday, it was all here. To choose one was impossible. Before long, the pile of possible choices was 30 photos deep. He added another photo to it and as he did, a small gust of wind sent the pile all over the floor. He looked over to the window, but it was closed. Maybe it hadn't been the wind; maybe he had bumped the table.

Moving his chair back, he bent down to pick up the pile and noticed one photo had slid away from the others and now sat alone, face down, under the table. He picked it up and turned the photo over. There she was, the sun setting behind her, her hair blowing gently in the sea breeze. Her smile looked beautiful and her blue eyes seemed to twinkle. This was the photo. This was how he wanted people to remember her.

'It's a good choice.'

The voice came from the window. He looked up and for a brief second he saw her reflection. He moved to go to her, but before he could get there she had gone. He stood by the window with his hand flat against the glass. He cursed his brain for playing these cruel tricks. More than anything, he wanted to feel her touch one more time.

He ate a small dinner and sat watching the world move outside his window, until it was time for bed. Lying in the dark he felt tiredness take over. He lay on his side with one hand on the empty space beside him. On the edge of sleep, he heard her voice so clearly. 'Good night my love.' A single tear ran down his cheek in response.

She died on a Monday.

Wednesday

His daughter approved of the clothes and the photo he had chosen. She let him know that the priest would visit later to get information about Elizabeth and her life. They talked about a couple of stories they would want told and what hymns they would like sung at the funeral.

Between her and his son they had arranged everything. The funeral was tomorrow at 11:30. A large turnout was expected and the wake would take place at the apartment. While the funeral was taking place, the caterers would set up everything. He thanked them for all the work they had done, apologised for not being more help, and for the first time he asked how they were feeling. They talked about their mum and how much they missed her. They spoke of times spent together and for the first time in two days he allowed himself to smile, even to laugh a little.

Later in the afternoon, the priest arrived to go over the funeral plans. The order of service was finalised and his son left to get it printed, with the photo in pride of place on the front page. They gave the priest information, so he could sound like a family friend when he spoke tomorrow. It dawned on him that they could literally have told him anything and he would say it. It made the priest's role seem almost irrelevant. He was no more than a middleman between this world and the next. He would speak fondly of a woman he didn't know and everyone watching would know it was fraud.

They were not a religious family and the priest had made a couple of comments about their lack of appearances at church. The family of the church would have liked to know them better, and maybe now they would at least get to know him and be there to support him. He smiled in response, saying nothing. His daughter thanked the priest for his time and showed him to the door.

He could hear them chatting as they made their way down the hall. He turned to the window and there she was. This time she was standing in the room, looking out towards the city. She turned to look at him and smiled. The front door being shut distracted him and by the time he looked back, she was gone.

His daughter offered to help him pick out a suit for tomorrow, but he told her he would be fine. They hugged at the door and she left, promising to be back first thing.

Walking back to the living room, he stopped in his tracks. He could smell Elizabeth's perfume. It was all around him. The light floral scent, unmistakably hers. He stood, breathing it in. He closed his eyes and imagined her there in the room.

After several minutes the scent left and he opened his eyes. Remembering he had to choose a suit, he walked to the bedroom and opened his wardrobe. Smaller than his wife's. Choosing a suit would not be hard. He had a choice of two. He brought them both out, laying them on the bed. One black, and one charcoal grey. Black was traditional, although she had always preferred him in the charcoal suit. She said it made him look handsome. That was all the reason he needed to put the black suit back. Next was the choice of tie. Should he go with traditional black, or with something more colourful? She had always liked him to wear some colour, even at funerals. The dead might enjoy seeing colour when they say goodbye she had said. Who wants a sea of black to see you off to the light? He chose a blue tie with no pattern. Some colour for her, but not overly daring. She was the outgoing one, the free spirt, he was more conservative. She said he worried too much about what other people thought. She was right; he did worry about little things that now seemed trivial.

He laid the tie next to the suit and took out his best white shirt. The outfit was completed with a pair of black shoes, his only pair. They looked a bit scruffy and would need to be polished. Leaving the clothes on the bed, he took the shoes through to the kitchen to retrieve the shoe polish from under the sink.

He was hit by her scent as soon as he walked into the living room. This time though, as well as the scent, he saw her. Sitting at the table, in the chair where she had died. She looked up and smiled, before vanishing before his eyes. He dropped the shoes to the floor and began to cry. He knew he wasn't going mad, he was seeing her, smelling her and hearing her. She didn't seem ready to leave and he wasn't ready to let her go.

Composing himself he picked up the shoes and walked over to the table. Setting the shoes down, he got the polish and sat across from her chair. He placed an old newspaper under the shoes. She didn't like him polishing his shoes without protecting the table. He polished the shoes in silence, staring at the space where she had been. There was no scent now and she didn't come back. One thought went through his head, over and over as he worked on his shoes. I miss you.

'I miss you too.' The voice came from everywhere and nowhere. He turned around but no one was there. The tears came again as he lowered his head to the table.

She died on a Monday.

Thursday

The day of the funeral. The day he would say goodbye to his love. The day they would put her in the ground and place a stone with her name above her final resting place. A small consolation, a reminder to passers-by that she had been here, she had mattered to people. She had touched lives, created life, and now was gone, but never forgotten.

He showered and dressed before his daughter arrived. His son would be coming with the funeral cars she told him. His daughter straightened his tie and sorted the collar of his shirt. She absently brushed some specks of dust off the shoulders of his suit, smiling sadly.

They sipped coffee while waiting for the cars. Neither seemed ready to speak of what today would hold. As if not speaking about it meant the events of the day may not unfold. He stirred his coffee for the fifteenth time, watching the patterns the spoon made as it distorted the surface of his drink.

The buzzer sounded and his daughter walked to the receiver. She lifted it; said hello then nodded her head. She turned to him and smiled sadly. It was time. He took a deep breath, composed himself and stood up. He walked slowly towards the door, realising he had not been across the threshold since Elizabeth had gone.

His daughter held the door open and he put his hand out to take the weight of the door. She moved down the hall towards the stairs and he turned to shut the door. Elizabeth was sitting at the table. She smiled, waved, and then vanished.

He stood, frozen, for a few seconds. His daughter called out to him, and the spell was broken. He moved towards the stairs, one step at a time. Each step, a step closer to a final goodbye. Each step taking him further away from their home, from the place where she still seemed to dwell. What if the funeral, the very act of putting her body to rest in the cold darkness of forever caused her to leave for a final time? Was he ready for that? Could he be without the brief glimpses of his love? He almost turned back, but fought the urge and continued towards the car. Not going to his own wife's funeral because he believed her still to be present in their apartment was not a conversation he wanted to have with anyone.

He sat at the window in the back of the car, his daughter and son next to him. No words passed their lips. All three lost in their own thoughts about what lay ahead. He became so completely consumed in his thoughts that he didn't notice the car stop, or the church looming over them. When he was finally shaken from his dream-like state by his daughter's gentle hand, he looked up at the church. For a house of God, the building seemed unwelcoming. It towered above the cars and the people waiting outside.

They were ushered inside and made their way to the front row. The family of the deceased should always sit at the front, to show their grief to the world. It wasn't enough that the love of his life was gone. He now had to march up the central isle while friends smiled and nodded their heads. Some reached for him as he passed. Keeping his head bowed he walked on, without making make eye contact or acknowledging anyone.

The priest took his place above them in the pulpit and the service began. He told stories of Elizabeth, just as they had planned. Like an old friend reminiscing fondly, he talked of a life, fully lived, but taken too early. Of trips planned and never taken, of the mysterious ways of God, whose plan we shouldn't question, but should just accept, until one day everything will make sense, when you believe.

At this moment, today, here in this church, he was finding it difficult to believe. To believe in a God that would take his Elizabeth away with no warning, with so much left undone and unsaid. Where was the planning in this? Where was the hidden hand guiding them towards the great unknown, the ever after? Where was the divinity in this act?

The tears began to run down his face, as his heart drowned in the unfairness of it all. Despair swept over him once again, his reason for living had been taken from him and, if there was a God, then they were a God who didn't care about him.

The service continued with more stories. His son read a passage from the Bible. This was the first time his son had opened a Bible, never mind read from one. They sang hymns that were vaguely familiar and then it was over. Coffin bearers carried out Elizabeth and the congregation gathered again at the freshly dug grave.

Standing by the side of the grave, with the rain pouring down, and the wind battering umbrellas this way and that, he watched as the coffin was lowered into the ground. His daughter on one side, his son on the other. As the coffin continued down, they moved closer together, as if each was stopping the other from collapsing.

Finally, with the coffin laid to rest, the priest threw some dirt on the lid, while saying a prayer he had said a thousand times before. His son stood forward, picked up some dirt and did the same, his daughter next. Then he found the strength to move and picked up the cold wet dirt. He looked down at the coffin, paused for a moment, and then let go. The dirt struck the coffin with the sound of hailstones hitting a window.

With the tradition complete, he stepped out of the way as others followed. All looking uneasy and unsure. Was there a right or wrong way to throw dirt? Each looked to the congregation after their turn, seeking confirmation that their dirt throwing was done respectfully.

He turned his head away from the grave and his eyes scanned the graveyard. Grey and dark in the heavy rain, the clouds gathered above them, blocking out the sun. Rows and rows of headstones, marking the place other people had put their own 'Elizabeths' to rest.

As he continued to look at the vast graveyard, he saw her in the distance. A woman so out of place. No raincoat or umbrella, she moved freely and easily between the graves. A flash of colour on an otherwise grey landscape. He kept watching, transfixed by this woman who was getting closer and closer. Elizabeth. As the rain poured down and the wind flipped umbrellas inside out, she continued to walk towards him. Her clothes were the clothes he had buried her in.

The rain had no effect on her; the wind was not able to move a single hair on her head. She smiled as she looked at him.

His daughter noticed him looking off into the distance. She held his arm giving it a gentle squeeze. He looked to her, and then back to where Elizabeth had been. She was gone.

Back at the apartment, people came and went, letting him know how sorry they were. Sad smiles and light touches on the shoulder. The occasional hug and comments about how it was so unfair, too soon and too young.

He was grateful for his children. They moved among the throng of people, thanking them for coming, and doing most of the entertaining. Was that the right word? Could you entertain on the day you buried the love of your life? Interacting seemed too cold a word, entertaining seemed too light, wrong in some way.

'Does it matter?'

The voice, her voice, came from right next to him, inches from his ear. He turned but no one was there. He smiled briefly. He didn't suppose it did matter. Whatever you called this, no word was right.

The appropriate amount of time for people to linger uncomfortably must have passed, as one by one they said their goodbyes and left. Each small group that departed created more space, less sound, and less cover for others. You could sense the unease, as no one really knows how to act in these situations. The trickle became a stream, until there was no one left. His son and daughter began tidying up. Dishes were removed; uneaten food was wrapped in foil and placed in the fridge. Trays were piled next to the tea and coffee jugs that the caterers had left. They would return early next week to collect them. His daughter had written that on the calendar next to the fridge. When he looked at her scribbled note, he realised that this was the only event on his calendar that would take place. Other entries, in Elizabeth's handwriting, would now be left incomplete or unattended.

His children left, the apartment was clean and there was nothing for him to do. His eyes returned to the calendar. Elizabeth had always been a planner, a photograph taker, a ticket stub collector, a recorder of information. She had boxes of photos and mementos. None held value apart from that of a sentimental nature. He used to tease her, telling her that she spent her whole life looking forwards or backwards, that she didn't live in the moment. She said that was his excuse for being disorganised.

'Well, I was right, wasn't I?'

He turned to see her standing by the radio. She didn't disappear this time. She stood, looking perfectly alive, staring back at him. He froze, not wanting to move, in case he averted his gaze and she vanished like a cruel magic trick.

'I'll always be close by. You don't have to be sad. I'm not in any pain.'

He smiled, unsure how to respond. He didn't want to tell her that he was in great pain, it seemed selfish. He wanted her to come back to him, not in fleeting appearances or ghostly visits.

She smiled a smile he had seen one million times before, the smile he had fallen in love with all those years ago. Tears filled his eyes, blurring his vision. He wiped at them, looked up and she was gone. Come back he thought, please come back.

She died on a Monday.

Friday

He woke in his bed, unsure how he had got there. He didn't remember going to bed, didn't remember anything after Elizabeth. Sitting up, he looked at the empty space next to him. Reaching out his hand, he touched the pillow lightly. The clock on the bedside table said 8:15. He had slept in, but not by much. When he thought about it, he didn't have anything to do. Can you sleep in when you have no plans to be late for?

His children wouldn't be coming over today. This would be his first day of being alone, truly alone, since Elizabeth had died. He convinced himself to get out of bed, showered and dressed. He spent the next hour or so wandering around his apartment. His apartment? Is that how quickly theirs became his? He admonished himself for the thought. It was their apartment, not his, theirs.

After opening and closing the fridge for the tenth time and deciding that he wasn't hungry, he wondered how he would fill his day. Elizabeth would always have something planned, some chore that needed done, or an activity they would do together. Whether it was going for a walk or doing a jigsaw, it was done together.

He looked out of the window. The rain was still coming down, that ruled out a walk. Jigsaws had always been more Elizabeth's thing; she had the patience he lacked. He could read a book, he had several in his 'to be read' pile on the bookshelf. Sitting down on their couch in their apartment, he opened his chosen novel and tried to concentrate.

He read the first line five times, each time it appeared to read differently. The thoughts in his head kept playing over and over. Is it ok to do something normal in such an abnormal week? Is it ok to enjoy reading so soon after his wife, his love, had passed? Was he going through the motions of existence until…? Until what?

'You can't think like that.'

He turned to see her sitting at the kitchen table. The book dropped to floor, diverting his attention for just a second. It was enough for her to be gone. Was he seeing her? Was she here?

'I'm here, I'm wherever you are.'

The answer came from everywhere. He looked all around but couldn't see her. He looked all over the apartment, their apartment, but she wasn't there. Come back he thought. He waited for a response. This time, none came.

He moved to the kitchen table and waited. Not sure what he was waiting for, he waited. He wanted to see her, to talk to her, smell her scent. He wanted something, another connection. Anything, he wanted anything at all. The surprise and joy each time she spoke to him or appeared in the apartment was equalled only by the piece of his heart that died each time she left.

After an hour of waiting he decided she wasn't coming back today. Standing up, he went to retrieve the book he had discarded earlier. As he reached for the book, her scent consumed him. Every breath was her. It was like walking into their bedroom when she was getting ready to go out. Beautiful and comforting at the same time. He breathed deeply, reaching out his arms as if he could embrace the scent, keep it to treasure somehow. He smiled, but at the same time tears ran down his face.

He crumpled to the floor next to their couch. Lying on the carpet, breathing in Elizabeth, he fell asleep, one hand reaching out, stretching for something just beyond his reach, yet always nearby.

He was woken by the radio. Elizabeth's favourite station, playing her favourite music. The smell was gone. As he sat up, dazed and confused, not remembering how he came to be on the floor, he looked for her. She was not here.

'Answer the phone.'

Her voice came so clearly it shook him from his dazed state and he realised the phone was ringing. Trying to clear his head, he got to his feet and picked up the receiver. His daughter was calling to make sure he was ok, to apologise for not seeing him today. He managed to convince her that he was fine. Being alone was what he needed. They had a short conversation during which she reminded him to eat. Had he had dinner?

Had he had dinner? How long had he been on the floor? He looked to the clock, 7:15. He had been on the floor for hours. Hours that felt like minutes.

'You need to eat.'

The voice came from the kitchen. He looked over as the fridge door fell open, but Elizabeth was not there. He rummaged through the remains of the buffet, finding enough to resemble a dinner. Cold chicken, cold sausage rolls and an egg sandwich that had begun to harden, but was edible. He washed this down with some relatively fresh orange juice.

Dinner had always been a time to be together. He loved to cook and Elizabeth would help, or get in the way as he called it. They talked and laughed while their little world filled with the smell of the meal. It was always a special time. The hardened egg sandwich, congealed chicken and rubbery sausage rolls seemed like a fitting meal to have; now she wasn't with him.

'See, you did need my help after all.'

Her voice came from behind him. He turned to see her looking into the fridge, which was still open. I need you to do it wrong so I can show you how to do it right, he said in response. She smiled then appeared to fade in front of his eyes.

He felt the tears well up, the tear as his heart broke once again. How many times can one heart break? She didn't return to him that night. He waited, he looked for her, he spoke to her. He turned on her favourite radio station. He sprayed her scent, stared at her side of the bed, but she didn't come back.

She died on a Monday.

Saturday

Weekends were always full of things to do, people to see and time to be well spent. He reminded himself of this as he stood in his pyjamas staring out of the bedroom window at the scene below. People going back and forth, this way and that. Busy in their own lives. He watched as they moved below him, each on their own path, each with a purpose, with a goal. What was his goal for today?

'Get out the apartment. Go for a walk.' Her voice came from the ensuite.

He looked into the empty bathroom. Her scent was subtle, but there. She was not. He decided to take the advice; maybe a walk would do him good. The fresh air couldn't hurt.

The effort it took to become motivated surprised him. Every step in this seemingly straightforward task became a challenge of both mind and body. Finally, he was dressed and ready to step outside. He opened the door but didn't move. He stood staring at the hallway, the boundary between their world and that of everyone else.

He breathed deeply, and then stepped forward. One foot after the other, each step a personal achievement. He had no idea where he was going, no plan. He kept walking, out of the apartment, out of the building, on to the street and among the people. Each stranger he passed had no idea of the pain he carried with him. Was that selfish? He didn't consider their pain, why should they consider his?

He made it all the way to the park. His body had entered autopilot and brought him here. There had been no intention to end up here, but yet, here he was. They loved this park, especially at this time of year. The leaves on the trees were a beautiful mix of oranges and reds. The ones that clung to their branches outnumbered by those that had given up the fight and fallen to the ground. The piles of red and orange irresistible to passing children, who jumped and kicked their way through them, smiling and laughing.

He found their bench, the one with the best view of the lake, while also being sheltered from the wind by the trees that stood guard behind it. He sat down and watched the water. The small ripples moving across it. A group of men huddled together as their remote-controlled boats moved effortlessly across the lake. A shared hobby, a common bond that brought them together. What were his hobbies? Did he have any? Who were his real friends? Did he have any? Had he become so dependant on Elizabeth that without her his life was one of solitude?

'That's ridiculous and you know it.'

He turned his head and there she was, sitting next to him on the bench. Was it ridiculous? How many of their friends were his friends?

'They need time, just as you do.'

I need you he thought.

'You'll always have me.'

With that, she was gone. He was left alone on the bench watching the men and their boats. The tears moved down his face. He didn't wipe them away; he left them to find their own path. If any passers by noticed he was crying, they didn't let on.

He stayed that way for some time. Watching the men, crying on and off. He wondered why he kept seeing Elizabeth. Was she so much part of his world that if he finally let go forever, that world would collapse? Or was he simply not ready to say goodbye? Was the way she had been taken so cruel in its swiftness that he felt robbed of some process, some feelings he should have been prepared for?

The suddenness of Elizabeth's death had ripped him from his world of comfort, love and happiness and thrown him into a life of uncertainty, of hurt, of despair and fear.

He was scared to face the world without her. Scared of waking up every morning and remembering that she wasn't there. He feared spending each day wondering when she would appear or speak to him. Scared, most of all, of the day she finally stopped.

He made his way home, avoiding eye contact with the world. His eyes still stung from the tears. He welcomed the rain that had begun to fall. It masked his tears. His bloodshot eyes were not the focus of the people passing by. Their focus was firmly fixed on getting to their destinations as dryly as possible.

Finally, he arrived at his apartment, the rainwater dripping off his jacket, his trousers uncomfortably damp. His shoes were, apparently, not watertight, as his socks could testify.

Sitting on his bed he slowly stripped off his wet clothes. Not bothering to dress again, he found his dressing gown and wrapped himself in it. The warmth of the cotton against his skin felt good after the cold and damp. Lying down on the bed he drifted in and out of sleep. He had not intended to go to sleep, but his body had other ideas.

As he lay in warmth and comfort, the exhaustion consumed him. Grief had stolen his energy. His eyelids became heavier, eventually shutting off the world around him. Deeper into sleep he went and as the last strands of the world disappeared, he heard her voice.

'Sleep my love.'

She died on a Monday.

Sunday

He woke with a start. He felt uneasy, scared even. He didn't know what had caused that feeling, what had ripped him so suddenly from sleep. Looking to the clock, he saw that it was 8am. He had slept for over 12 hours. He remembered coming home, getting changed and then being on the bed. He didn't remember sleep hitting him like a brick wall.

Gathering his senses, he made his way through to the living area. Her scent filed the room, it was unmistakable. She was with him. There, at the window, he saw her reflection, as if she was standing in the room looking out. There was no-one standing where she should have been and yet her reflection was clearly visible. He walked over and stood next to her. Looking at her faint image in the glass.

'I miss the views.'

Her voice was clear and strong.

So why don't you stay? Why leave all the time? I miss you.

'It's tiring, being here takes energy.'

He looked at her reflection, it flickered as she spoke. He reached out to the window and touched the glass. She did the same. Her hand touching the other side of the glass. His smile was one of sadness; a single tear ran down his cheek. I miss you.

'I miss you too. Not being here, in this place, with you is the hardest thing.'

Then stay, he said, looking into her eyes.

'I can't.'

With that she was gone. Her reflection flickered. Her eyes seemed to fade first, and then she left. Emotion swept over him. Tears spilled from his eyes. He let out a barely audible moaning sound. The pain in his chest grew, his heart felt like it could burst at any moment. He curled on to the floor. Heartbroken, and defeated. His sobbing continued, his body shook, and the pain of his broken heart grew.

She had died on Monday and every day since, another part of his soul had died. He had tried, yesterday, to be normal, to go to the park and take part in life. Being around people without her was something he still couldn't contemplate, not really, not now, maybe not ever. The effort it had taken had driven him to exhaustion. She had died on a Monday and he wished it were him.

The sound of the door being unlocked made him sit up. He quickly tried to compose himself. Wiping frantically at his eyes and nose, straightening his dressing gown, he went to stand but found the effort too much. Instead he sat, legs bent, knees to his chest and waited for the uninvited visitor to appear.

He heard his daughter shouting for him, announcing herself. Heard her footsteps as she looked for him. Heard the change in her voice when she saw him. His daughter ran to him, kneeling, placing her arms around him. The shock and sadness in her eyes at seeing her dad in this state was what finally made him move.

He told her over and over that he was ok. It had just been a hard morning. There were good days and bad ones, and this was a bad one. He explained, unnecessarily, how much he missed his wife. His daughter moved position and sat against the wall with him, their backs to the windows, and placed her head on his shoulder. She held his hand gently, wrapped her other arm around his, and they stayed like that. No more words just the love of someone who shared your grief.

Someone who had lost as much as you. Someone who understood, almost completely, how you were feeling.

Eventually he felt strong enough to stand. His daughter helped him over to the couch and went to find some food or at least some tea. He looked out towards the hall and there at the bedroom door, he saw Elizabeth. Just for a second, she was there, then gone. He remembered what she had said. It was tiring coming to see him. It took energy she had said. Did that mean she would need to stop? Was this brief glimpse all she could manage?

His daughter saw him staring out towards the hall. She followed his gaze but could see nothing. She had found enough food to make a sandwich; the offerings from the caterer were now passed their best. She had placed it all in a binbag, ready to be thrown out. She put the sandwich and a cup of tea down on the table by the couch. A plate for each of them.

They ate and sipped their tea in silence. She was relieved to see her dad eating. He was relieved that she couldn't see his heart breaking. The pain was constant. He made a mental note that he would need to get better at hiding his pain from the outside world.

After eating, his daughter tidied up the kitchen, went through to the bedroom, and he could hear her making the bed. He was grateful for her help. The pain in his heart continued, it felt heavy in his chest, too heavy. As if his chest could no longer bear the burden of carrying something so broken. He sat there, unsure what to do. He stood up on shaky legs and walked through to the bedroom. His daughter was now in the bathroom tidying. He watched her from the doorway, reminded of how much she looked like her mother.

His daughter looked round and caught him staring. She came over and hugged her dad. A gentle kiss on his forehead. She asked again if he was ok. He said that he was and hoped that she was convinced. She had her own pain and didn't require his to be placed on top of it.

She stayed for another hour, seemingly unwilling to leave. Three times she asked him to come and stay with her. Just for one night, it would do them both good. When this was rejected, she offered to stay at the apartment with him. He reminded her that she had her own family, her own responsibilities. Finally, she was convinced enough to leave. She hugged him tightly at the door. The pain in his chest grew, but he said nothing. The door closed behind her and for a brief second everything went black.

'You should have told her.'

He turned to see Elizabeth walking from their bedroom to the living room. He followed, expecting her to vanish at any second.

'She has enough to worry about,' he said, as he absently touched his chest, aware the pain was subsiding.

Elizabeth sat down on the couch. The flickering had gone, she seemed stronger. Her presence more real than before. He sat next to her. Still she stayed.

'I miss you. I miss waking up with you. I spend each day waiting to see you, smell you or hear your voice. I spend each day terrified that I won't see you. Then when you do come to me. I worry that you'll go too quickly. My heart breaks every day and every day it seems impossible to live without you.'

She reached out and to his surprise, he felt her touch. The feeling of love that coursed through his body was overwhelming. The smile that came to his face was real, as was the joy that filled his soul. He placed his hand on hers. She smiled back at him.

'How?' Was all he could manage.

She pointed towards the hall. He looked to where she was pointing and caught his breath. There, halfway up the hall, was his lifeless body. He looked to her, confused, questioning.

'Now we will always be together,' she said, squeezing his hand.

No long lingering illness. No last words, just there then gone.

He died on a Sunday.

ACKNOWLEDGEMENTS

As always there are other people to thank for helping with this story, and the artwork. First of all, I would like to thank Shirley Husband, who's eye for detail, grammar and punctuation far surpasses my own.

I would like to thank the Beta readers who gave their time and their thoughts. Thank you to Sarah, Rebecca, Audra and my own mum. Their feedback and thoughts gave me the confidence to continue my first project away from my usual genre.

The cover design is by Theresa Bills, who showed patience and professionalism through my countless revisions.

Printed in Great Britain
by Amazon

67430941R00029